The World's
Shortest Stories
of Love
and Death

* * *

ALSO BY STEVE MOSS

The World's Shortest Stories (Editor)

The Book of the Few (Editor)

GroanerZ (Editor)

Inconsequential Journeys

The Coffee Book

The I Chew

ALSO BY JOHN M. DANIEL

Play Melancholy Baby

The Love Story of Sushi and Sashimi

The Woman by the Bridge

One for the Books: Confessions of a Small Press Publisher

Structure, Style, and Truth—Elements of the Short Story

The World's Shortest Stories of Love and Death

* * *

Passion. Betrayal. Suspicion. Revenge.
All this and more in a new collection of amazing
short stories—each one just 55 words long!

Compiled and Edited by
Steve Moss and John M. Daniel
Illustrations by Glen Starkey

RUNNING PRESS
PHILADELPHIA · LONDON

Illustrations by Glen Starky
Cover and Interior designed by Mary Ann Liquori
Edited by Patricia Aitken Smith
Typography: Trixie and Garamond Light

This book may be ordered by mail from the publisher.
Please include $2.50 for postage and handling.
But try your bookstore first!

Running Press Book Publishers
125 South Twenty-second Street
Philadelphia, Pennsylvania 19103-4399

To Daphne and Fatso

CONTENTS

PREFACE

When I was a teenager, my older brother's wife complained to me that she could never get his attention when he was playing the guitar.

"I swear," she said, "he loves that guitar more than he loves me."

Years later, they got divorced, which turned out to be a happy ending for both of them.

You've just read a 55-word story. Not a good story, I admit; in fact, it may be the worst story I ever wrote, and is certainly the worst one I ever read. All it has going for it is that it's true, which is a lame excuse for a story. It's just a bit of family history, best forgotten.

Oh, one other thing it has going for it: It's short.

Many years later in 1987, my wife and I were honeymooning in San Luis Obispo, California, when we came upon a copy of *New Times*, a weekly newspaper, edited by Steve Moss. In it was announced a new writing contest, 55 Fiction. There were a number of rules, but it boiled down to this: Contestants had to write a complete short story with plot, setting, and character, all within 55 words.

Great gimmick, I thought, and then thought no more about it.

A few weeks later on a hot, full-moon, Santa Ana night, I found myself unable to sleep, as newlyweds sometimes are, and so I got out of bed, dressed, and took a walk around the neighborhood. As I walked, I got to thinking of my brother's first marriage, and I decided to write the whole story of that marriage in 55 words.

I figured at that length, I could write it in my head and have it written before I returned to bed, which I did. It took about fifteen minutes.

In the morning, I took my story, still in my head, to the office and keyed it into MacWrite. That took about ten minutes. I counted the words and found I had written 237. It took me over two hours to pare down the story to 55 words.

In the process, something magical happened. As I threw away words, the story grew. The shorter it got, the more alive it became. It got better and better and peaked at about 60 words. I threw away five more, just to qualify for the contest, and the story was still good.

In throwing away words, I had thrown away the family history and had told a greater truth in a small pack of lies. Even though—as they like to say in Hollywood—it was based on a true story, it had become fiction.

Moreover, to my surprise, I had written a story about love and death.

I once heard author Herbert Gold say that all great literature is about love and death. He went on to say that if you disagreed and told him you could name a piece of great literature that wasn't about love and death, he would be happy to demonstrate to you how it was about love and death, or that it wasn't great literature.

I agree with Mr. Gold. Of course, love and death can be packaged in many ways: deathless love, loveless death, the death of love, the love of death. . . . The point is, love and death are what matter in great, great literature. They are what matter in great, small literature, too.

Whether or not my story, "Guitar," is great literature is questionable, but it made me the widely published author that I am today. Before that story, I had published only a few dozen short stories in literary zines whose average circulation was about room temperature.

I entered "Guitar" in the New Times 55 Fiction contest, which had more readers than I'd ever reached at one time before or since. I won first prize, which included a T-shirt and an award certificate. Since then, the story has taken off. It was reprinted in *Publishers Weekly*, then in a collection of my short stories, and eventually in the book, *The World's Shortest Stories* (Running Press, 1998), edited by Steve Moss, not to mention the audio edition of the book (*Listen & Live Audio*, 1998).

I learned three things from this success story, and I routinely pass them on to my writing students. I now pass them on to you.

First, write small. Words that don't matter are fat; write lean.

Second, forget what really happened. Writers of fiction should trade in their memories for a good imagination.

Third—and most important—write about love and death.

John M. Daniel

INTRODUCTION

We had no idea such a tiny idea could ever get so big.

If you're familiar with our first book, *The World's Shortest Stories* (Running Press, 1998), then you've already been introduced to fantastic flights of 55-word fiction. We'd asked people to write a story in just 55 words. We asked them to pretend that all they had was a ballpoint pen and a Post-It™ note to write upon. Make it fun. Make it crazy. Make it sing. But be sure to make it short.

And they did. That first book caught the imagination of writers around the world, bringing stories to us from England, Japan, the Philippines, Italy, Canada, and other far-off regions of the globe.

The result is this new book, which carries on the tradition of compressing big ideas into small wonders.

The hardest thing about writing a 55-word story is that within these tiny confines, something has to happen. Then it has to lead to a satisfactory conclusion so it feels complete. Sounds relatively easy, but it's not. If you'd like to give it a try, check out the back of this book for our guidelines.

One thing we've noticed as the genre has evolved is that writers have been raising the creative bar, often breaking out of more traditional narrative. Can a complete story be told in a cooking recipe? Sure it can. How about a funeral invitation? No problem. There's even a three-act play here and a tale told with half the words intentionally missing.

Love and death are the themes in this book, and from two simple words, writers have let loose their imaginations: Let's go meet some aliens from beyond the stars, then jump in a time machine, encounter witches and vampires, head back to the Garden of Eden, seek love in cyberspace, take a moment to have sex on Venus, murder our spouse, flee some cannibals, and stop by Alpha Centuri on our way to the afterlife, while watching the end of the world on network television.

Writers have done it all here. In just 55 words.

There are even parodies of famous works. Two stories might need a quick explanation for those unfamiliar with the tales they poke fun at.

In O. Henry's 1906 short story, "The Gift of the Magi," a poor young couple buys Christmas presents for each other. She sells her long, beautiful hair to a wig maker to purchase a watch chain for him, and he sells his watch to buy combs for her hair. "Oh, Henry!" on page 44 takes up immediately after the original story ends.

Then there's "The Britches of Madison County" about a woman who has an affair over a weekend when her family is out of town. On page 140, we discover how it might have been written on the bestseller list in an alternative universe.

And this time, we decided to ask several well-known personalities to try their hand at writing a 55-word story. Cartoonist Charles

Schulz obliged, as did TV producer Norman Lear. Writers Herbert Gold, Neil Steinberg, Barnaby Conrad and science fiction maven Larry Niven did, too.

We thank them, and all the other writers who took up the challenge to engage readers utterly in what has become an endlessly inventive sub-genre of the short story.

I'm going to shut up now and let you read some great stories. I've already spent over 500 words telling you things that aren't half as interesting as what writers here have done in one-tenth that space.

Steve Moss

Falling
in
Love

* * *

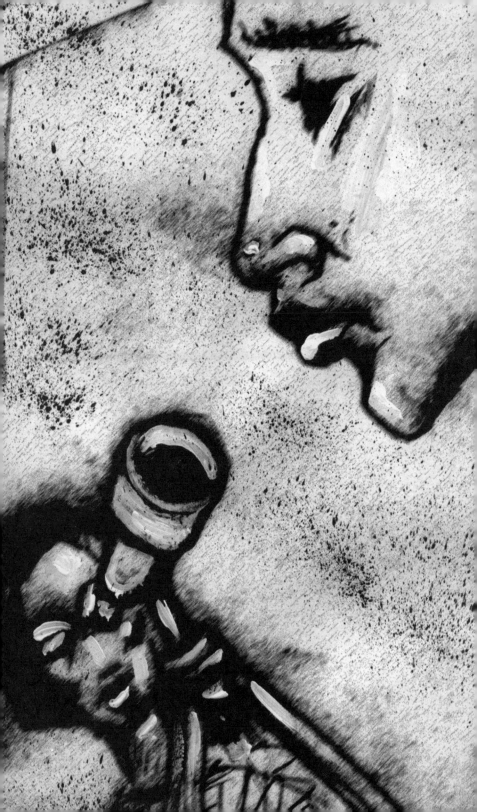

HUBBLE TOGETHER

She loved him.

He didn't know.

She wanted to tell him. She didn't know how.

"Isn't it sad," she said, "how the stars are so cold and the sun so warm."

"The stars," he said, "are just farther away."

"Can they get closer?"

"... Closer?"

"Yes," she said.

He looked at her.

And there was light.

WILLIAM S. HOWE

THE FOOL WHO INVENTED KISSING

He clubbed her and dragged her off to the cave.

She hated him.

He washed her face, untied her, and gave her the last meat from the fire.

That was better.

Hungry himself, he licked her greasy fingers, then her face. His lips brushed hers, paused, touched again.

Tomorrow, he would kill meat for her.

DOUG LONG

GOING OUT, IN STYLE

"Come on, buff your boogie boots. Let's go out dancing!"

Ricky and I had been buddies since third grade. But not until this night did we really meet.

Above the door in green neon blazed, "Beef Stew," the only gay bar in our hometown of Honeyrock, Kentucky.

Going in was my coming out.

SEAN CHRISTOPHER

NEW KNOWLEDGE

The serpent tempted Adam instead of Eve. Adam succumbed and Eve refused to eat the forbidden fruit.

The moment he chomped down on it, he knew that Eve was naked as sin. He lusted for her while she remained cool to his advances.

Finally, however, human curiosity won and she, too, had a nibble.

Revvvvvelaaaaation!

MICHAEL DRIVER

RAINY NIGHT PEOPLE

Wet walk to beach-side dives. Clothes dry, dendrites soak in liquor. Bad karaoke.

She was ahead; damp, window-shopping, puddle sloshing. Discussing things with herself.

Devoured midnight eggs and potatoes with a foot on his thigh. Both thirsted touch.

Foreplay on shiny, black, deserted streets enroute to his dump with an ocean view.

GREGORY MORELAND

THE LIFEGUARD

I eyed that chick all summer, and she never looked my way.

Strutting around the pool, twitching her butt, adjusting her top, drinking Cokes, ignoring me . . .

Then one morning, she almost drowned. I blew my whistle, dove.

As I carried her out, she squirted water in my eye and laughed, "Thought you'd never notice me!"

D. RAY RAMSEY

THE IMMACULATE ASSUMPTION

He assumes she knows.

She assumes he doesn't.

Based on this assumption, she assumes he'll understand. He assumes she will, too.

They agree to meet in a downtown cafe.

He assumes she knows the time.

She assumes he knows the place.

Hours later, they part ways. Both of them assuming the situation will resolve itself.

ALAN ROBERTS

Easy Come, Easy Go

She'd zealously guarded her virginity, so he'd stood her up on Prom Night.

Years, later, he's come downtown to see her new film.

Now, he watches her image on the screen, realizing his mistake. She has undeniable talent. He should've stood by her.

Suddenly, the screen goes dark. He searches his pockets for more quarters.

Shannon O'Rourke

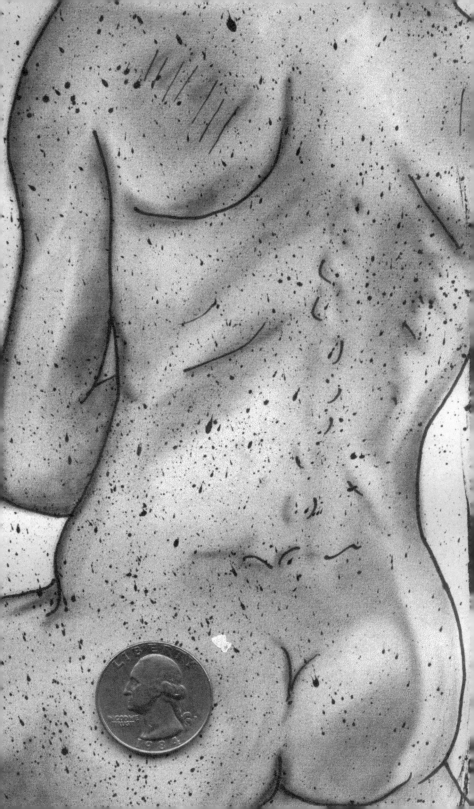

OFFICE PARTY

"Come in, honey."

Standing, he hugged her. But then the phone rang.

"Yes!"

Irritated.

"He's early. Tell him about ten minutes. Hmm?

Mmmmmmmm! Good! Very good! ... Yes—yes!

Wonderful! Honey, go out that way. Sorry about

your dress. On you, it still looks like a million bucks.

... Yes, tell Mr. Arafat I'll be right there."

TONY CAMPION

THE QUESTION

Starry night. Perfect time. Dinner by candle light. Fancy Italian restaurant. Little black dress. Beautiful hair, sparkling eyes, feminine laughter. Together two years. Wonderful times. True love, best friend, no one else. Champagne. Marriage proposal. On one knee. People stare. So what? Lovely diamond ring. Blush. Beautiful smile. No?!

LARISSA KIRKLAND

TRUTH IN VEGETABLES

"The afternoon light through the motel curtain oranged her hair. He reached again for her thigh.

"Don't go."

"I must."

"Or what?"

"I'll turn into a pumpkin."

"Yeah, right."

"I wouldn't lie to you. I'm a vegetarian."

She inched out the door.

He tried not to think about the green tendrils curling beneath her dress.

TOM EWART

LATE CHARGE

He had so many secrets, so many charms. Each time they were together, it was better than before. She loved the way he smelled, the way she held him, her hands caressing his spine.

She brought him back to his place, and paid the librarian for keeping him out too late.

Again.

JENNIFER SAYLOR

A Dream Is a Fetish
Your Heart Makes

T' wasn't her face—beautiful, but so what?

Nor the gown. The place was full of low-cut gowns.

How boring. But those transparent shoes . . .

Feet! Ooooo, feet!

Alone with her in the garden, I whispered,

"Dance . . . ?"

"Please be careful. Breakable shoes."

"Take them off," I crooned.

She laughed, bending to make my dream

come true.

LEE TYRON

THE WINNER

The casino was crowded, but Brent saw only Ellie. He had to win . . . for her . . . for her love. He dropped his last three coins in the slot, and pulled handle. The reel spun; no win. He slumped onto the stool. "I've lost everything.'"

"I love you," she whispered.

His heart leapt.

Jackpot!

DOROTHY G. OLSON

FOREVER STAR CROSSED

"Come on, kiss me—nobody's watching."

The young couple embraced.

"We shouldn't meet like this."

"Says who?"

"Everybody. My family doesn't like you. My mom says you're not right for me."

"Yeah, mine too. But who cares?"

"I sure don't. Because I love you, James."

"And I love you, too, Gary."

CHRISTINA DIAZ

LOVE, HERE IS THY STING

Fate decreed that these two people, blessed with beauty, brilliance, charisma, and yearning for love, should be walking toward each other on the seashore this idyllic morning.

They noticed each other's beauty, but passed without speaking.

She didn't like guys.

He didn't like girls.

Fate giggled, then went on gaily about her business.

WALTER E. HOPMANS

REUNION

Clearly, they connected. Each sensual rendezvous culminated in a new shared ecstasy. Their energy forged new passion into their separate lives.

Daily, they met on-line in virtual anonymity. Identities were superfluous.

"You are delicious," she typed.

"And you are my sweet marmie," he gushed.

She laughed. "My son used to call me that.."

"MOM???"

"DAVID???"

LINDA KENNEDY FLOYD

ALL SHE LEFT
WERE HER COOKBOOKS

Break two hearts, carefully separating centers; add wine sparingly. Adjust psyche; froth. Melt inhibitions; bake on high uncovered on sheet. Dot with climactic release of wonder.

Add sweeteners, exotic praises, hope, and leftover emotions. Sprinkle remaining broken hearts on top, followed by a splash of bitters.

Serve cold.

Toss most discretion out and begin again.

CHRISTINE FINCKE

Living
in
Love

* * *

IN THE BEGINNING

She was mad at him. They had almost everything in their idyllic life, but she coveted the one thing they lacked. Only his cowardice stood in the way.

She would dump him, but she couldn't yet, so she would resort to cunning and seduction. Naked and beautiful, she grabbed the fruit.

"Adam," she called softly.

ENRIQUE CAVALITTO

AFTERMATH

A year after his death, she found the letters in the potting shed, addressed c/o his office. He'd been leading a double life; indeed, had apparently been running two homes.

Which now explained who that tall, elegant woman had been at the graveside ... and the child by her side wearing his unforgettable pale blue eyes.

DAVID CROSSLAND

O, HENRY!

They had exchanged Christmas gifts joyfully. It had all seemed so right at the time. And it made perfect sense, considering their current financial circumstances. Times were hard, yet love prevailed.

But then he had a sudden thought: "Her hair will grow back, but my watch is GONE!"

Outside, the harsh December snow fell.

JEFFREY SCOTT BAKER

X-Rayted Version

Grinning, Lois wrote the invitation. She put on her red dress and prepared: perfume, candles, martinis, soft jazz . . .

Clark came home exhausted from leaping tall buildings. Didn't notice the candles or music, gulped his martini, looked right through the dress . . .

. . . read the invitation taped to Lois's belly . . .

. . . and felt himself become a Man of Steel.

BILLIE BATSON

OF PROOF AND PUDDING

"Prove that you love me," she said.

"Okay ... No more sex."

"How will that prove it?"

"Because I'm giving up what I want."

Later, when they went to bed, she kissed him tenderly. They made love.

"You weren't going to do that," she said afterwards.

"It's my reward," he said, "for proving I love you."

L. G. HUNT

LETTUCE PRAY

Okra Winfrey rushed to the hospital.

"Your husband's been creamed," Dr. Beets told her.

Okra was boiling mad.

"Can't you do any butter?!" she screamed.

"Quiet, peas! He's in the operating room now!"

said the nurse, who was steamed herself.

"Here he comes!"

"Well?"

"Success! He'll be a vegetable the rest of his life!"

CATHERINE S. ROMEREZ

LOVE NIGHT ON VENUS

The Venusians decided it was her turn to have the child—Lucren had carried the last.

Removing her shacquran, Messen received Lucren's dronse. Messen saw the blue planet on the horizon. She closed her eyes.

Lucren was good. Messen was satisfied.

Opening her eyes, she looked again into the sky.

"The earth moved," she whispered.

TONY CAMPION

TIME AND MONEY

He was a workaholic at 20; wealthy by 30.

"Time is money," his dad always said. "Keep your nose to the grindstone, your eye on the buck."

At 38, his business collapsed. His wife left him. He became critically ill.

Recovered, he admires sunsets and tells his children, "Time is time; money is money."

DOUG LONG

FAMILIAR AS FURNITURE

That night we danced as strangers, crazed with curiosity, seems like ages ago. Now we sit together, comfortable, like this old sofa. Is our love a carefully cultivated tolerance of withered passions? Perhaps it's the truest of all.

But letting my night robe slip free before you, we begin to remember that night we danced.

SEAN CHRISTOPHER

BATTLE OF THE HAIKU SEXES

"Write a haiku in seventeen syllables," she commanded.

"Can't be done," he said.

"The Japanese do."

"And they lost the war, didn't they?"

"Irrelevant," she murmured.

"Women, that feminine logic," he complained.

"Here's how," she said. "Repeat SHUT UP eight or nine times."

"That's either sixteen or eighteen," he said. Smugly.

HERBERT GOLD

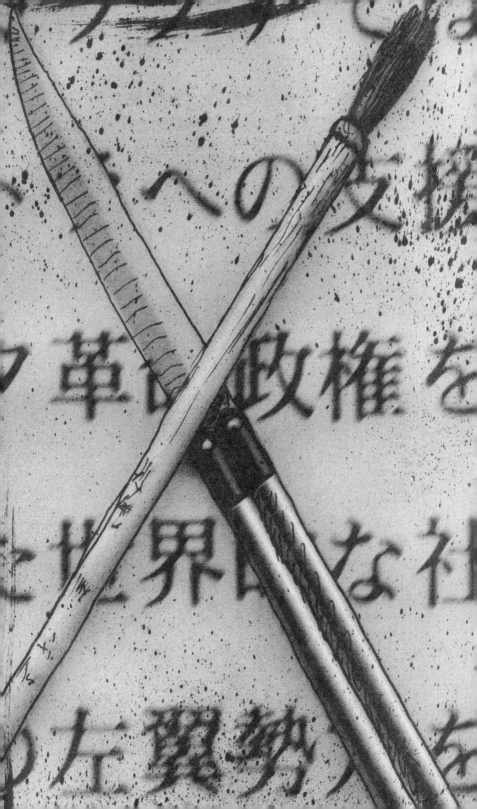

ERRING DIRTY LAUNDRY

Dirty laundry covered the floor.

"Is it sorted, Jim?" Linda demanded of her husband.

"Sordid?"

"Yes, sorted," repeated Linda. "It's not a trick question."

Jim froze, terrorized.

"It's all so dirty," Linda grumbled.

"Honest, Linda," Jim stammered. "It wasn't sordid or dirty. It was only an office infatuation!"

It all came out in the wash.

JOHN DAVIDSON

WE'RE STILL DRIVING IT

The sex was fabulous, furious fornication in the back seat of that green '69 Impala, high on Vegas and cheap tequila.

Not the honeymoon of my dreams, but hell, we're still together after 27 years, three kids, AA. Can't knock that. Although, come each anniversary, I'm inevitably swimming with the memory of slippery leather.

SEAN CHRISTOPHER

THE MISFITS

"Arthur, will you take this woman . . ."

Are you kidding? This calendar girl? Those world-famous bazooms? Move over Jack Kennedy, Frank Sinatra, Joe Dimaggio . . .

"I will."

"Marilyn, will you take this man . . ."

Well, duh. This guy wrote "Death of a Whatchamacallit," right? We're talking serious brains here . . .

"I will."

"Then I pronounce you . . .

J. D. KEPLER

MUCH MARRIED

The bigamist got off with two years community service.

"Eleven spouses is punishment enough," said the judge.

All of them turned up at the pub to celebrate.

A young man stepped through the crowd and lunged at the bigamist.

His deep, lustful kiss was met with matching passion.

Her eleven husbands welcomed the newcomer.

ROB AUSTIN

THE MORE THINGS CHANGE

When they met, her hair was wild, her name was Peace.

His hair was long, his name was Sam. He played guitar for her.

Sam traded his guitar for golf clubs.

She's long since cut her hair. He calls her Judy.

But sometimes, under a full moon's light, he sees Peace and kisses her anew.

CHRISTINE M. AHERN

DEBRIEFED

"Who said, 'Brevity is the soul of wit'?" she asked, looking up from her reading.

"Let me see if I can recall," he answered. "Could it have been Mark Twain? Naw, not homespun enough. Shakespeare? He wouldn't use one word where a dozen would do. Maybe Oscar Wilde? Hey, how about—"

But she had already left.

BILL CROWN

OSEPH
CONRAD
THE
Grapes
OF
Wrath
JOHN
STEINBECK
THE
OF
WILLIAM
FAULKNER

THE CATCHER IN THE NIGHT

I grumped to the nursery, leaned over the crib, changed the ammonia-perfumed diaper, then held his body to my chest, promising to protect him from the virus, if only he'd let me sleep.

Deal.

We both slept in the rocking chair that night. Next morning, I was the one with the cold.

No regrets.

MORGAN CHILDS

GEORGE AND MARTHA

A weary salesman's weekly homecoming.

"Welcome, George," says Martha.

Dinner and a cozy fire. Then to bed and sleep.

Downstairs, the cat knocks over a vase.

Half awake, Martha shouts, "Oh, God! My husband!"

The bedroom window banging open brings her full awake.

The bed is empty.

"George! Why are you out on the roof?"

STANFORD SMITH

THE MISSING LINK

She was Cro Magnon, he Neanderthal. Couldn't have kids.

A distant relative—erect, intelligent and mean—invaded their cave, killed him, raped her, and took off with their stuff, leaving her heartbroken, destitute, and pregnant.

Anthropologists wonder who he was.

Forget him.

He wasn't someone you'd want to know.

TAYLOR BINGHAM

Death
of
Love

* * *

ROUGH RIDE

"This is my taxi!"

"Like hell—I hailed it!"

They shared the cab. They started dating. Movies, dinners, weekends away. He proposed. She accepted.

She began to nag. He kept interrupting her.

It blew up one night.

"Let's call it quits," he said.

She nodded, looking around.

There was only a single cab in sight.

L. SOTH

PRACTICAL ETHICS

"You want me to see what she's up to?" I asked my new client.

"Yes."

"A photo would be helpful."

He produced one.

"Not surprised you're worried."

He tried a smile. Didn't work.

"Be in touch."

He left. I went home.

"Anything new?" Lois asked.

"Your husband doesn't trust you."

"I'm not surprised," she smiled.

PATRICK HERRINGTON

SENSIBILITY

Orderly. Efficient. Busy.

It was sensible. The day should so pass.

A file out of place. He pulled it, but it fell, spilling yellow letters and photos. He picked up a picture.

Kelly's bright smile shined from it—a face, a love from another time.

He filed it back in place.

Orderly. Efficient. Busy.

GARY BOURQUE

Ex-Girlfriend (Rach
Ex-Girlfriend (Suzanne)
Ex-Girlfriend (Kelly)
end (He

Top Bananas and Rotten Apples

ACT I
> Adam enters, alone.
> Eve appears, startles Adam.
> They talk.
> Eve offers bowl of fruit.
> Adam eats banana.

ACT II
> More talk.
> Adam decides to have an apple.
> Loud shouting off stage!
> They exit together, hurriedly.

ACT III
> Couple enters, wearing foliage.
> They talk. They argue.
> They exit.
> They live unhappily ever after.

CURTAIN

BOB BOLDT

AT THE HOSPITAL

She sped desperately. God, please let me get there in time!

But the doctor's face in the emergency room said everything.

"My husband!" she sobbed. "Was he conscious?"

"Mrs. Allerton," he said gently. "Be glad. His last words were, 'I love you, Mary.'"

She gasped, stared at him, then turned.

"Thank you," said Judith coldly.

BARNABY CONRAD

BAKE OFF

He studied her hair, flowing gently like molasses over her milky shoulders; her skin, as pure as the freshest shortening; her eyes, like delicate chocolate drops floating on pools of egg whites.

As Baker pondered just how he would lay lovely Cookie on the sheet, the knife slipped and dropped to his lap.

Foiled.

Forever.

BETH LONG

PLAN B

"So how do I earn the million bucks?" asked James.

"I have to pay alimony for the rest of my ex-wife's life, unless she gets married," said Frederick. "Can you help me out?"

"No problem."

A week later, the phone rang.

"Done deal," said James. "Pay up."

"Congratulations!" said Frederick. "When's the wedding?"

"Wedding?"

DORIS PARKLAND

GOURMET

She came, filling my house with the smell of cooking onions, and I learned the beauty of eating well.

Then she left.

I tried everything, even washed the walls with baking soda and tears, but I couldn't rid myself of her flavors.

Now I sit here, talking to you, undernourished.

RICHARD SHARP

AN UNSATISFIED CUSTOMER

"Let's talk," she says.

"Why wait?" I instinctively respond.

"I'm seeing someone else. A cooking timer salesman."

"For a limited time only?"

"I'm serious! He loves me!"

"Don't be fooled by imitations!"

"You watch infomercials all day. Every day. You're hopeless!"

"Act now, or else!" I challenge her.

"I'm outta here."

"But wait! There's more!"

ALAN ROBERTS

IT WAS A DARK AND STORMY NIGHT...

"You never take me anyplace," she complained.

"How can I on such a dark and stormy night?" he responded.

Their marriage was coming apart.

They were behind on car payments and the rent.

Their dog, Rex, decided he'd better take over. He sat down to write a bestseller.

"It was a dark and stormy night...."

CHARLES M. SCHULZ

Boxing Day

"Merry Christmas, Darling!"

"A beautiful box! What's inside?"

"Don't open it."

"Don't open it?"

"Never open it."

"Stop treating me like a child!"

"Do you want the box or not?"

Pandora nodded.

"Then don't open it."

She opened the box the next day.

The note inside said, "You're no longer a child.

I'm divorcing you."

MARGO BRAGG

BOOKED ON THE WEEKENDS

"Why'd you do it?"

Asked that same question six months ago, Tom told friends, "I married Karen to free up my weekends. No more driving six hours every weekend to see her."

Now the detective asks, "Why'd you do it?"

Tom looks down at Karen's lifeless body.

"I wanted to free up my weekends."

LAURA GETTING

LOVE BYTE

He looked up and nodded at her, his face
lit by the glow of the monitor. He didn't notice the
suitcase in her hand.

If only he had touched her half as much as
he touched that keyboard, given her a fraction as
much attention.

She sighed, wondering when he'd notice that
she was gone.

DARLENE LEFAIVE

CHEERS

The wine was a wedding gift. They vowed to save it for a special day.

The first child was born, then the second. The bottle remained unopened.

She got a promotion, but he was unwilling to share her joy.

When the divorce was finalized, they met to uncork the wine... it had turned to vinegar.

FRAN MANNA

So There

"Until you learn to give," he lectured, "you'll never amount to anything."

He left, determined to become somebody.

Eventually, she left too. She forgot him and taught the rest of her life at an inner-city school.

She'd hear of him someday, he vowed, even if he died young.

But she didn't. Even though he didn't.

J.M. Ferguson, Jr.

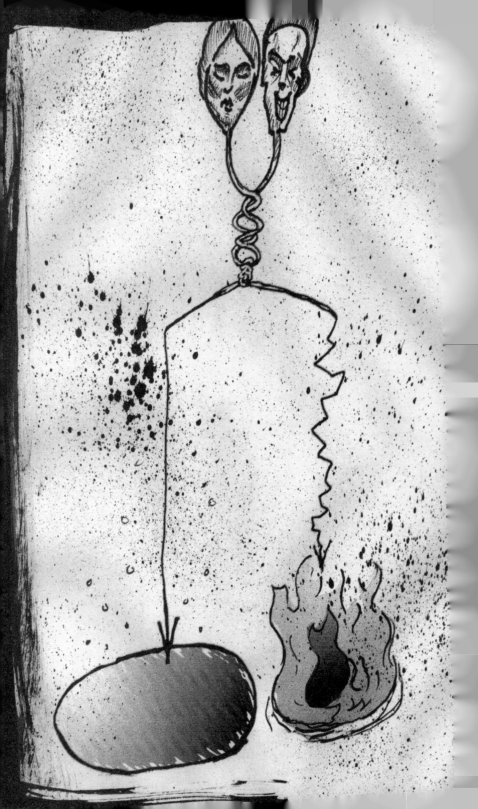

Love of Death

***

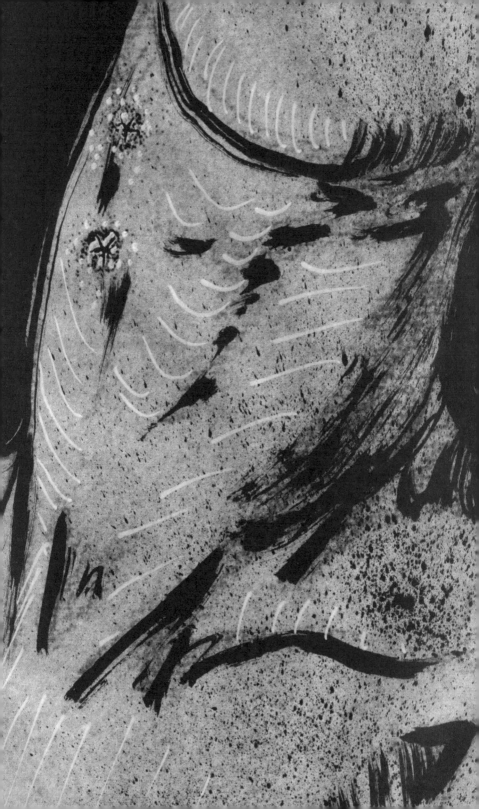

LOVE IMMORTAL

"My soul lost?" Her eyes questioned.

"To live immortal as my love." He held her closer.

"This tomb, damp and dark." Her eyes his.

"My world," he whispered, "you would see with new eyes."

"To never know sunrise again." Cheek to his.

"Moonlight strengthens love." Lips to her neck.

"Our love, immortal." Her love flowed.

DANIEL HAYS

DECISIONS, DECISIONS

The murderer finished off the last of the Candy Corn and regarded his victim's crumpled body.

"Neither guilt," said he, "nor fear of looming consequence dampens my enjoyment of this fine confection."

The doorbell rang.

The murderer raised his shotgun to the peephole.

"Who's there?"

"Pizza delivery, sir."

"Life," the murderer reflected, "is a test."

J.R. McCarthy

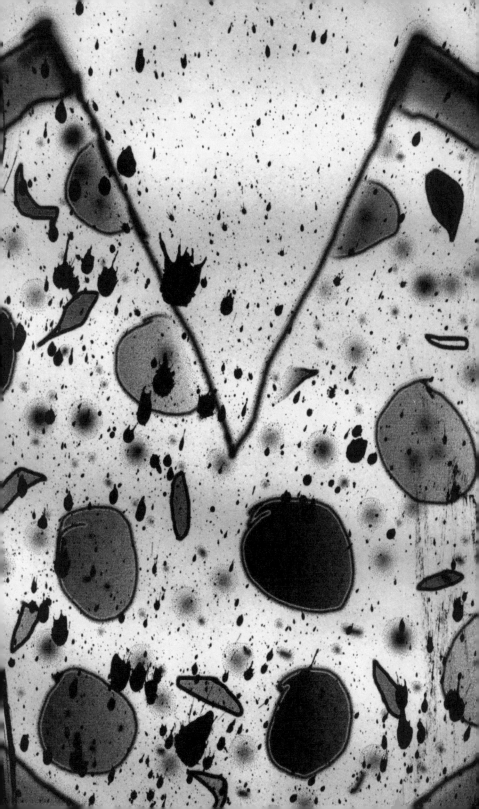

LAST WORDS

The suicide note was brief.

To my friend, my lover, my wife,

Don't blame yourself.

None of them did.

ROB AUSTIN

DEATH BECOMES THEM

Cyanide was quick, arsenic tasteless.

She had prepared the food with great care, making his favorite dishes.

He was a genius at mixing perfectly balanced drinks.

"Dinner's ready," she called.

They sat opposite each other.

She served them both.

He proposed a toast.

"To life!"

She raised her glass to her mouth. He began eating.

MINOTI SAHU

LOOKING AHEAD

"In the woods. Alive."

She gives the exact location.

"Thank you!" The parents, in awe, rush from the room. The father pauses.

"I'll leave your check on the table."

The psychic nods.

"That's fine. Now go to your child."

He leaves. Another door opens.

"What now?" a voice asks.

"Snatch another kid," the psychic instructs.

CHERYL L. LEFLAR

THE PROMISE

She slowly lowered herself into the hot, swirling water, remembering his promise that the spa would ease her aches and pains.

He had been buried a week ago and her pain was great.

She acted swiftly, with determination. As the water turned red and the world around her blackened, she nodded.

He was right.

CAROLE ADAMS

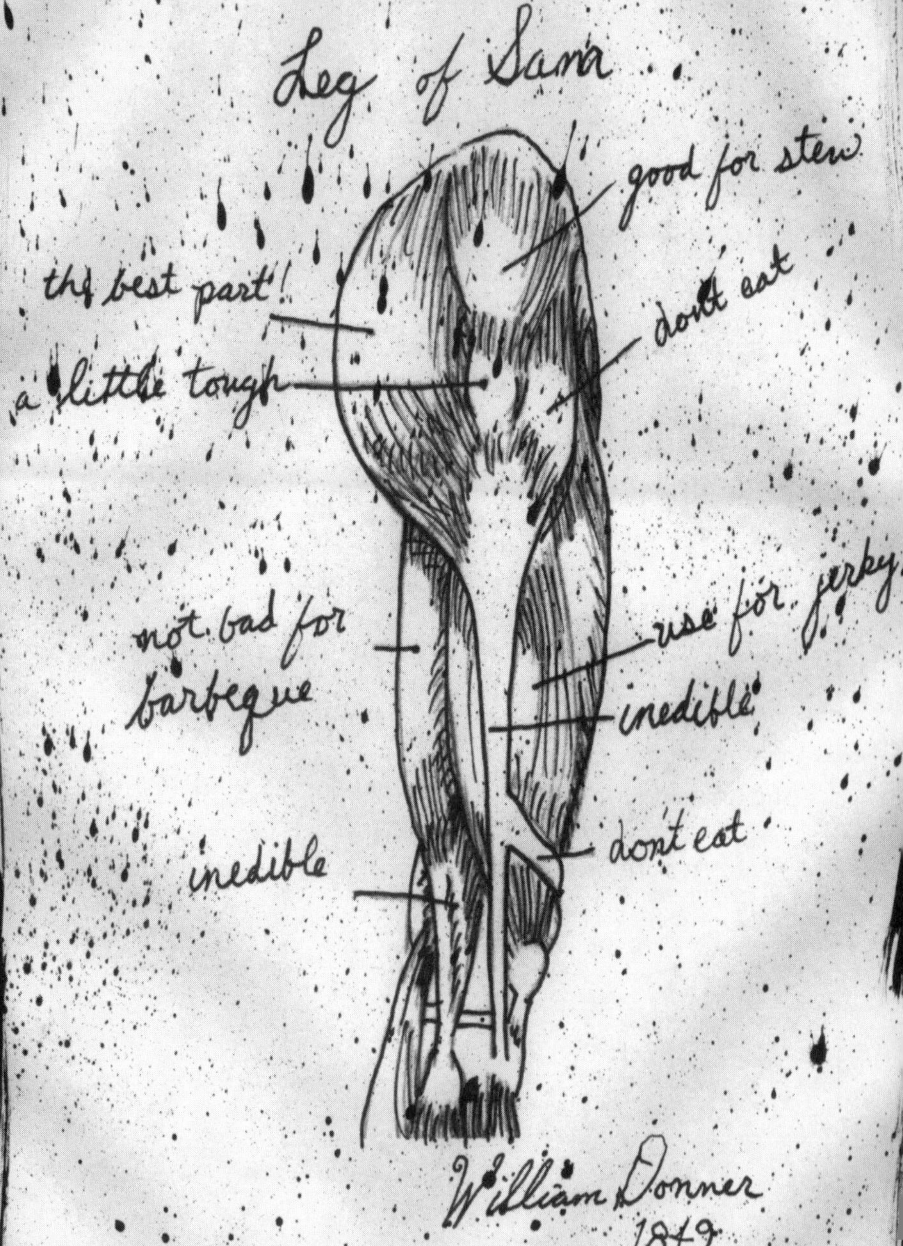
Leg of Sam
good for stew
the best part!
don't eat
a little tough
use for jerky
not bad for barbeque
inedible
don't eat
inedible
William Donner
1849

BON APPÉTIT

7:15

"No reservations? Sorry. If you'd care to wait for a larger table . . . "

7:45

"My apologies. Still nothing available . . . "

8:25

"Donner party of eight? Your table is ready. Oh, only five of you now? Just dessert tonight? And toothpicks? Very good, sir, right this way . . . "

KATHERINE POEHLMANN

PERFECT OPENING LINE

A dozen bodies of women with slashed throats.

Never a sign of forced entry.

Detectives were baffled.

Meanwhile, the slasher was on the prowl again.

"Piece of cake," he sneered.

Knock, knock.

"Go away!"

"Your husband's with my wife tonight! Please! We have to talk!"

Door opens abruptly.

Works like a charm, as he grabs her.

BETTY FINNEY

Wisdom

"Give me your wisdom."

"Willingly!"

The djinn's despairing howl became a wild laugh.

The djinn said, "Now you may go where magic fades and a djinn would die. Return in time and share our mind again."

"But I'm mortal!"

The djinn reached into the man.

Better. But what a fool he was.

Not any more.

LARRY NIVEN

FINAL ARGUMENT

She rolled over next to her husband, feeling a little guilty about today.

"Honey, I'm sorry. It was all my fault, and it should never have happened."

If only he wouldn't take everything so seriously. She snuggled closer and put her arm around him, then wondered why he felt so cold.

"Honey . . . are you . . . alright?"

GARY T. BURGESS

THE KIDNAPPER

Bob covered his mouth to disguise his voice over the phone.

"You want to see your daughter again, it'll cost you fifty thousand!"

"Deal!" replied the voice on the other end. "But if you want to see your son back, it'll cost you sixty!"

Bob slammed down the receiver.

For him, crime just never did pay.

DAVID MORRIS

THE TRUTH AT LAST

"Thanks for coming. Since I'm about to die, I thought you might finally believe . . . that I didn't do that to your daughter."

James leaned close to the glass partition before replying, "Luckily, only you and I know that."

James smiled and left to join his wife, and wait for their daughter's killer to be executed.

PATRICK LAWLER

Marie:

Your love me[ant] everythi[ng]
to me. I don['t bl]ame you,
I always figu[red someday y]ou
realize how [wor]thless I a[m]

Sorry abo[ut] the mess; [I]
couldn't stay [to] live any
longer. Bu[t y]ou'll always [be]
[w]ith me.

Glenn

[P.]S: The f[...] I served you[r]
[to]night w[as] poisoned. Se[e]
[soo]n.

THE SUICIDE NOTE

Marie:

Your love meant everything to me. I don't blame you, though. I always figured some day you'd realize how worthless I am.

Sorry about the mess; I just couldn't stand to live any longer. But you'll always be with me.

Glenn

P.S. The fish I served you tonight was poisoned. See you soon.

ERIC SANDBERG

TEMPTATION

"Whosoever drinketh shall thirst no more," the glowing visage intoned, holding forth the goblet. The crowd stared, frozen in awe.

One dared step forth. He took the goblet, drained it, collapsed, clutching his throat. Soon he stopped thrashing.

The crowd gasped in horror as the visage darkened.

"Did I lie?" he sneered, vanishing in smoke and laughter.

ERIC SANDBERG AND CHRIS HANSEN

THE MASTERPIECE

Hypnotized by his handiwork, the arsonist felt sedated by the burning hillsides. He took it all in—the smell, the roar, the flying embers, the orange inferno he had created. He felt warm all over.

Too warm. Dreamily, he felt his legs burning . . . Suddenly conscious, he screamed as he became part of his own masterpiece.

KAREN ROBLES

LET'S MAKE A DEAL

Vanna pranced across the television screen. "I'd kill for a body like hers."

"That could be arranged," offered the cherubic man on the adjacent barstool. "Say . . . one murder per fortnight?"

"I accept your terms, sir," she laughed, ordering another martini.

Crushing the pedestrian on her drive home was an accident.

The first time.

PAUL RAYMOND MARTIN

UNDYING LOVE

Vacationing on their 50th anniversary, Frank and Helen stood with friends above the rushing river with its boiling rapids.

Helen slipped, fell, and was swept into the waters. Without hesitation, Frank plunged in after her. Both perished.

"He should have known he couldn't save her."

They watched the river roar.

"He knew."

ARTHUR W. COATS

Death
of
Life

* * *

LIFE STORY

"Push! It's a boy!"

"Melvin, school!"

"Hello, Susie."

"Do me, Melvin!"

"We're pregnant?"

"Dammit, I'm pregnant!"

Dear Melvin, Susie's lawyer's letter began.

"Come here often?" asked the bar girl.

"How much for the whole night?" said Melvin to the streetwalker.

"Football injury," Melvin told the stranger in his bed.

"Heart attack," said the coroner.

KEN GOLDMAN

THE FIRE NEXT TIME

The letter was ridiculous.

Her adopted daughter—a witch's offspring? Evalina was obedient, did her homework promptly.

"Mama, is that letter about me?"

"No!" she said as she placed Mrs. Crosswell's letter in the fireplace.

Across town, Mrs. Crosswell—social worker, Maples County Adoption Agency—in her bathtub watched, astonished, as her body burst into flames.

ANONYMOUS

ESCAPE CLAWS

The little girl watched as the bony kitten played outside her window. Quietly, carefully, she opened the window and patted her hand on the brick below.

The kitten ran to her, stretching its front paws just below her fingertips.

"Meow," the kitten cried, wanting in.

"Help me," she whispered, desperate to get out.

ADEENA DWORKIN

LAST WORDS

"Alive!" she cried.

"What?"

"My husband!" she gasped. "We just passed him! What did you do?"

"What you said—even remembered to set the timer."

"You dropped it off at the front desk for Victor DiMauro?"

"I thought you said, 'Leave it for Victor tomorrow.'"

"Fool! Where is it now?"

"Don't worry. It's right h—"

KATHLEEN HENNESSY

UH-OH

Such a tragedy! Oskar Wellington killed in the accident, leaving Elena a childless, young widow. Her consolation: She was now free to spend Oskar's multi-million-dollar fortune all by herself.

But at the service when the minister called for the widow Wellington to approach the pulpit, 17 women followed Elena up the aisle.

MICHELLE BAGA

WHODUNNIT

The murderer had to be someone in the room.

"I can prove I was at the hairdressers until after three," declared Miss Pinkerton.

"I was out playing golf from eleven onwards with Reverend Carruthers here," maintained Colonel Smithers.

All eyes turned to me...

"Oh, don't be ridiculous!" I cried. "I'm the butler, for goodness sakes!"

DAVID CROSSLAND

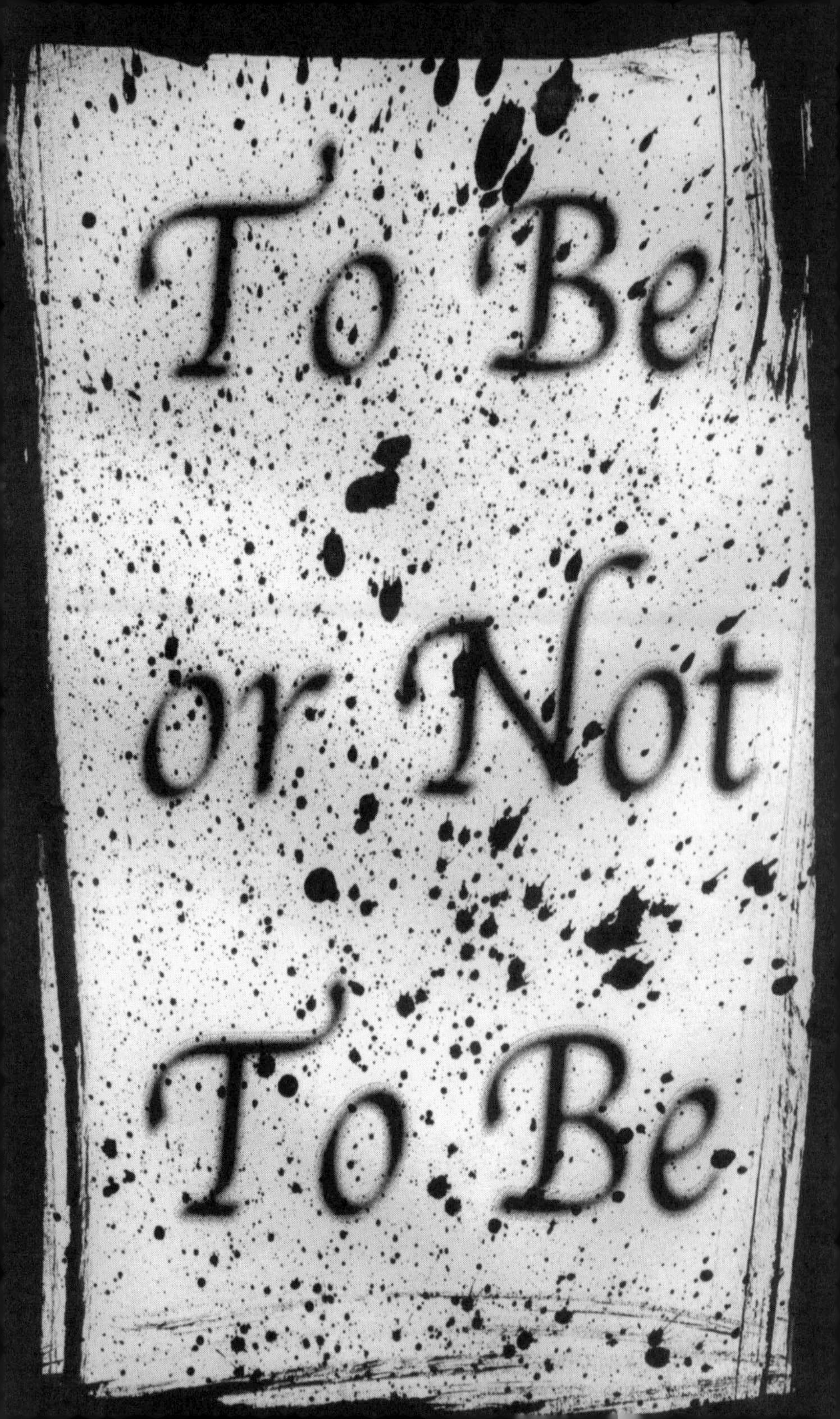
To Be
or Not
To Be

GERTRUDE'S SOLILOQUY

My son and husband never got along. The boy seemed to blame Claudius for his father's death. Claudius suggested prep school. Who needs a kid moping around the house?

Now Hamlet's back. He's worse.

Claudius isn't much better. "They teach you philosophy, boy? Nihilism? Ever consider suicide?"

Those two. They'll be the death of us all.

PAUL HENNEPIN

THE RECKONING OF ROPE

I never noticed before the bristle of rope until it pulled snugly about my naked neck. Why all this cheering? Surely they harbor secret sins. Yes, I regret raping in a drunken fury, but no one asks if she shared the same rage. The floor has fallen beneath my feet.

SEAN CHRISTOPHER

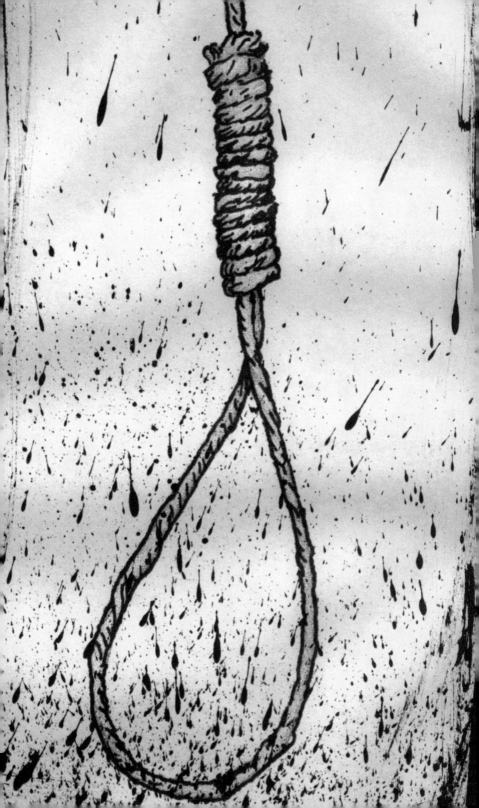

NO ONE'S FAULT

"Why do you go so far?" Sally Jesse asks Jerry.

"I give them what they want," says Jerry. "Besides, Geraldo's worse."

Geraldo enters and says, "I am not. You are despicable."

Howard jokes, "You, my friend, put the 'spic' in despicable."

In Florida, two children shoot their father's fiancée.

"Done. Who do we call first?"

ALAN ROBERTS

UNOBSTRUCTED

Her wrinkled face sagged with pity. Such a nice,
young couple. At least they'd seemed so when they
bought the lot in front of her. But such an extravagant
two-story house! Ashes and embers now.

She folded the matchbook thinking, "I just can't
abide rudeness."

Sighing, she rocked, watching her sun set over
the Pacific.

SHEREE PELLEMEIER

DEATH ON THE HIGHWAY

The deer's yellow eyes freeze in the darkness.

We collide and now my headlights reveal dust and the

downed animal—its muscles tense, legs flailing, trying

to support its wounded body.

I didn't want this to happen. His fur bloodied as I

kneel to gaze into dying eyes.

Bright headlights around the corner. I freeze . . .

JEFF WEIT

THE CLIMB

Three men started climbing 90 floors. The elevators were out until Monday, and Sam had to have the papers over the weekend. As they hiked the towering flights, the men busied themselves telling sad, painful stories. On the 90th floor, Sam's story was the most painful.

"I forgot the key," he gasped, then dropped dead.

NORMAN LEAR AND BEN LEAR

CLONE HUNTERS

His partner watched him holster his gun.

"How'd you spot him?" she asked.

"Didn't you notice his face? All the cuts? Probably never replaced his razor blade. Renegade clones always screw up on the small stuff."

"You're right—"

She shot him through her raincoat pocket.

"—and in three years, you should've bought a new tie."

BILL CROWN

SILVER BULLET

Sales were down for the sixth consecutive quarter. Acme Munitions was going under. The losses were staggering.

CEO Scott Phillips couldn't understand why, but shareholders would blame him.

He reached into his desk and pulled out a revolver, placed it to his temple, and pulled the trigger.

"Click."

He'd start with the Quality Control Department.

BRADD D. HOPKINS

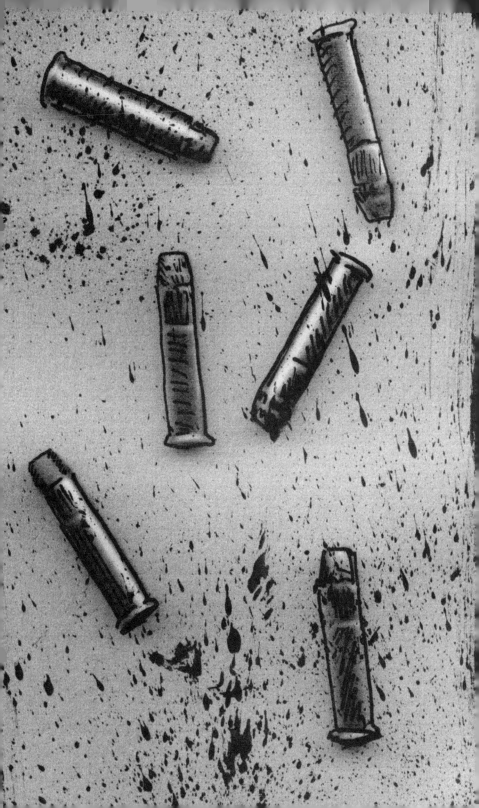

SUCH A DEAL

"A horse! My kingdom for a horse! I curse Bosworth Field and Henry!"

"Ah, excuse me, Your Grace ... "

"From whence did you spring, varlets?"

"Bernie, bring King Richard the horse."

"Yes, My Lord. 'Tis right here."

"A horse?! For me?"

"Indeed so, My Liege. Now, if you'll just sign here on the dotted line, please ... "

WILLIAM BOYER

A WALK IN THE WOODS

"It's time, old dog," sobbed the elderly farmer, chambering a round. Allowing no chance to lose his resolve, he quickly raised his gun and fired. The sound did not linger long in the woods.

The gray-faced dog pawed her beloved master for a few moments, then lay down to wait in her patient way.

WAYNE DIZE

To Air Is Human

Wrapped in bloody bandages, tubes stretching from his body, the accident victim gestured frantically to the attending priest. Desperate, unable to speak, he scribbled a message. Then, with a gasp, his breathing stopped.

After administering the last rites, the priest turned to read the dying man's final words: "You're standing on my air tube."

Trudy Flenniken

THE BRITCHES OF MADISON COUNTY

Francesca came out on the porch and welcomed them home, her husband, their son, and daughter. But her skirt was hung up in the waist of her drawers. The old man got hip and he shot her.

BILL CROWN

THE BUTLER'S REVENGE

He hopped into the kitchen, obese, leathery,

smelling like scum.

"Take me to the princess!"

"Sorry," I said. "This ball is formal."

"But she promised I could sleep with her!"

he croaked.

Welcome to the club. That little bitch.

I picked him up and put him on a silver tray.

"I'll present you," I said.

EVERETT STREET

FRIENDS

Jacob and Fowsi played together in a wide, shallow hole in the bright Mediterranean sand.

"My father is great!" said Jacob.

"My father, too!" said Fowsi.

"And we are friends."

"Yes, friends forever..."

"...And ever!"

"Shalom," said Jacob.

"Allah ysallmak," said Fowsi.

Then, faintly, across the settlements and the kibbutzim, the thunder of guns rumbled.

GARY BOURQUE

PATIENT, HEAL THYSELF

"He just stepped in front of my car!"

The investigating officer looked at the smashed hood and windshield, then the mangled body. He lifted a piece of paper from the dead man's hand.

"Thought it was a suicide note, but no..."

He handed it to the driver.

Sorry, I can't help you.

Sincerely,

Dr. Kevorkian

DEAN CHRISTIANSON

PRENUPTIAL ENCOUNTER

"Congratulations, Stephen. You're a very lucky man."

"Why, thank you, Michael. That's very generous of you, considering . . ."

"The history between Helen and myself?"

"Well, I . . . yes. Sorry, I didn't—"

"Of course not."

"Quite surprising, meeting you out here like this. I didn't think you—"

"Liked to hunt?"

"Yes."

"True. But this is an unusual circumstance . . ."

PATRICK HARRINGTON

THE STREETS OF LONDON

Rick waited impatiently at the intersection for traffic to clear.

"First time in London?" inquired a passerby.

"Yep," Rick replied.

"Need any help?"

"Are you kidding? I'm an American!" Rick said smugly.

"Righto."

"Nosey Limey," muttered Rick. He then looked left—no vehicles approaching—and stepped from the curb.

Last time in London.

JOHN DAVIDSON

TORTURE SESSION

A dirty, late-summer wind added to the tension.

"This should loosen up those lips," he said,

plunging a needle deep into an unsuspecting eye.

The recipient writhed in pain.

"Maybe you need a little heat."

Flames blistered the victim's flesh until death,

mercifully, arrived.

"Enough with you."

Tommy moved on to the next grasshopper.

STEVE ELLIOTT

tardunk's
666

Not Nightly Anymore

"Next on Nightly News, Apocalyptic horsemen run amok downtown . . ."

"This news brought to you by the great taste of Stardunk's virtual coffee! Ubiquitous Joe, your resistance is futile. Death, taxes—Stardunks!"

("*Live in three . . . two . . . one—*")

"Mephistopheles' gauntlet was thrown down today. At a town Stardunk's, the Devil led his horsemen, chanting, 'The end is—'"

GARY WALLEN

RED BEANS ANNE RICE

"Celebrate Mardi Gras with the oldest family in New Orleans," the invitation read.

I knocked on the door and was greeted by a plump, regal, raven haired lady wearing a purple velvet gown.

"Enter," she purred. "Come meet my family. We've been waiting for you."

Locking the door, she called into the mansion, "Dinner has arrived."

ROCHELLE LAPIN

DENIAL ON HIS LIPS

The smoker blows his smoke into the smoke-filled room.

"I love smoking," he rhapsodizes. "Smoking in a bar, smoking with my friends, smoking alone. I could smoke forever."

The phone rings.

He snubs out his cigarette. Smoke billows.

"Yeah?"

Pause.

"A spot?"

The cremation is short.

The pastor begins the service.

"Ashes to ashes. . . "

ALAN ROBERTS

RENDEZVOUS WITH THE KIDNAPPERS

Dad tossed the kidnappers the briefcase of money as they let me go. He drew backward away from them, his hand resting on a beeper on his belt.

But Dad never wore a beeper.

One raised his gun: "Sorry, we don't need witnesses."

Dad threw me down.

The explosion left little of them.

CHARLES E. BEACHLEY III

TYPE-A PERSONALITY

Yelkdslslweoh—Help me—iiiiiii I I I.....I cannnot breathe.......iiiiiiiiiii

2ioeriorey8erhiewikrejo#@#*jhreojojreojmlg;reg-porejorojojrojroprg909t4t0-4t1121=t000gggg--r9wp;up

Help me, please, somebody— please please help . . .

..k;;;;;;;; I am having a heart attack and there's nobody in the typesetting room except me---igsaj0u888o3p0-0

. . . I can barely move my fingerss to type this..[[Help me;;;;; help me help me helpppppppp meeeeeeeeeeee #@@#**

DANNY S. FAIRBANKS

153

THE ATHLETE

The crowd's roar was deafening. His eyes shut tightly, his arms reaching heavenward. Another defeated opponent at his feet.

He opened his eyes to a silent bedroom. Dusty silver trophies glimmered.

"What's happened to me?" he asked.

A chair creaked where he sat. The taste of metal made his tongue rigid. The trigger readied itself.

ALFRED C. MARTINO

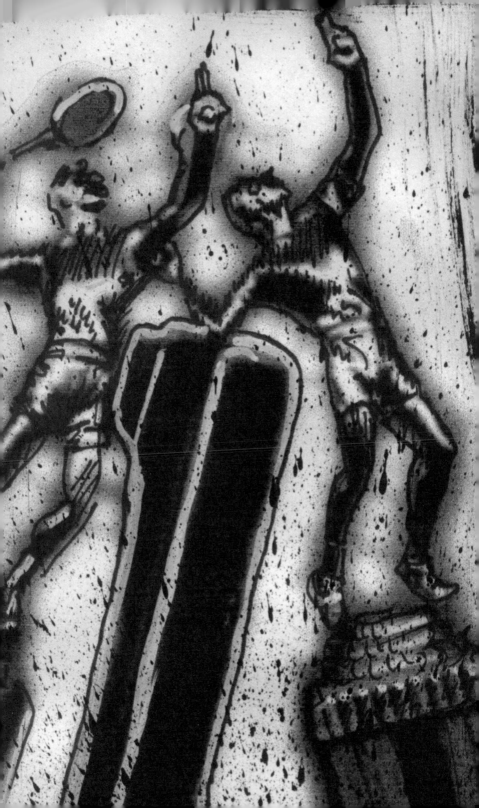

THE TRANSPLANT

Lying on the gurney, I felt the I.V. medications take effect.

"You came alone, right?"

"Yeah, Doc, just like you said. I get $10,000 just for a single kidney?"

"That's right, son."

Slipping into unconsciousness, I asked with slurred speech, "Then... why... all the... secrecy...?"

"Because I get twice that for a heart."

STEVE SAINSBURY

FINAL REQUEST

"Are his cement shoes dry yet?"

"Nope, but they'll hold."

"Then let's dump this stooge."

"Hey, guys, you're Vito Clamanzo and Tony Domenici, right?"

"So what? Shut up."

The police found his bloated body under water, cement on his finger. Inscribed at his feet were the names of Vito Clamanzo and Tony Domenici.

TOM STEFFORA

GOD'S MARBLES

"A nice one."

"Yes! And yellows make a bright flash when they bump!"

It held their attention. But they were growing bored.

The blue and green sphere with its swirling white spirals floated across the void.

Then there was contact, a quick vanishing, and the game was over.

EDWARD L. KING

PISTOLS AT DAWN

"We're here," the old Duke said, "to settle this dispute as gentlemen. As your only witness, I shall count your paces. One . . ."

On "two," Reginald DeCourcey spun and fired into the back of the man who'd slandered him.

Then, pointing his pistol at the Duke, he thundered, "Nobody accuses a DeCourcey of cheating! Witness that!"

THOMAS GRAHAM

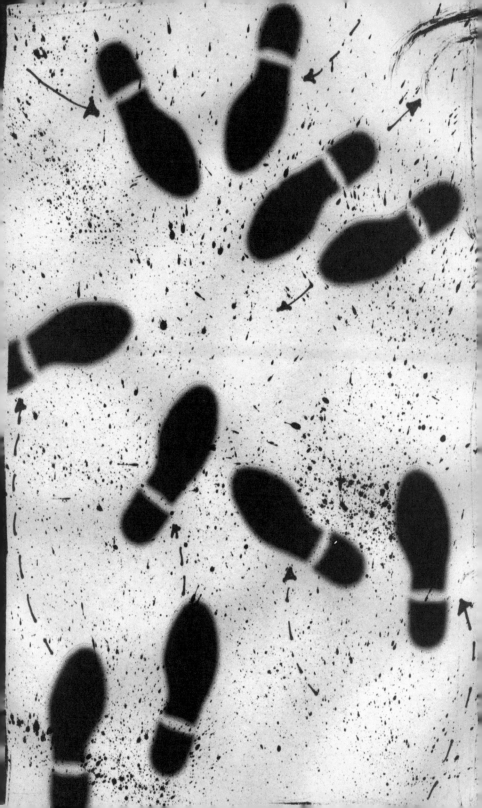

DANCE OF LIFE

Oh, how she loved to dance!

She plied through life, leaping over obstacles and tip-toeing past trouble. She spun through relationships, waltzed with lovers, jitterbugged with friends. She tangoed through youth and sambaed into old age.

And when she died, the story goes, her last breath expended itself with a bow.

CHRISITNE M. AHERR

GRACE

"Lord, thank you for this gift of grace. Making a cannibal chase me through the forest, You tested my faith. When I stopped running and knelt to pray, You gave me two miracles: deliverance from death and this convert who kneels beside me."

The missionary nodded to his companion. "Your turn."

"Lord, bless this meal..."

ROCHELLE LAPIN

Life After Death

* * *

THE TRUTH AT LAST

Saint Peter met me at the Pearly Gates.

"To enter, you must accept these truths: Jackie O. hired a hitman, the Earth actually is flat, and exercise causes cancer."

I accepted them.

"Oh, and another thing. . . O.J. is innocent."

"But the DNA!"

I agonize, sweating down here. But at least it's a dry heat.

R. J. FRIAS

CLOCK WISE

Old Man Barkley's bicycle rattles by my house every morning, six sharp, and has for the last 20 years. He crafts little clocks and politely peddles them in town. One of his finest sits on that stand, watching my bed.

Funny how it didn't chime today.

Skimming the paper at breakfast, I noticed his obituary.

SEAN CHRISTOPHER

FAST FORWARD

In the final three seconds, he saw himself blue,

then pink at his mommy's breast; crawling in diapers,

hugging his sister, playing, laughing, throwing a tan-

trum, going to school, fighting, swearing at mother,

crying at father's funeral, graduating, working, marry-

ing, stealing, being fired, divorced, drinking too much,

driving too fast, slamming into the oncoming truck.

DOUG LONG

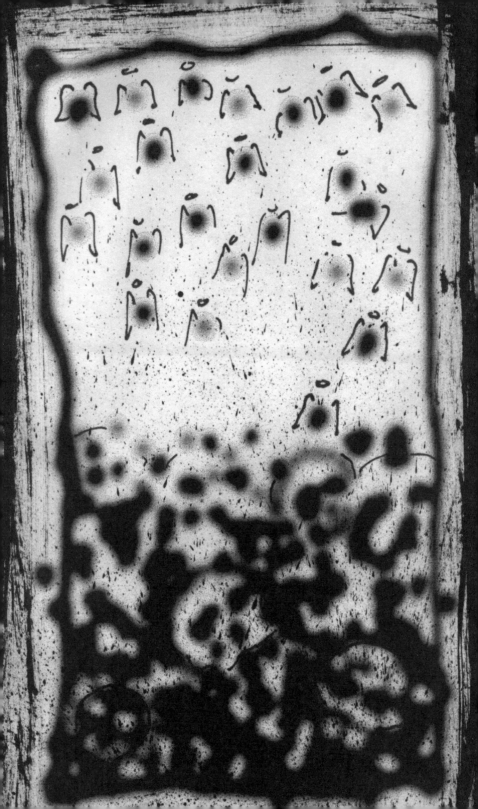

EQUAL DIVISION

A voice was heard between Heaven and Hell.

Who will take the doctors?

"I will," said the Lord.

"Who will take the lawyers?"

"I will," said Satan.

The sun was shining in Heaven. It was raining in Hell.

"I have my quota," said Satan.

"I have room," said the Lord.

JOYCE DEMOS

SALEM, 1692

Ropes cut the skin at my wrists and ankles. The town, gathered below me, chants, "Witch!"

I am condemned.

"Burn her!"

Sentenced.

As the flames approach the straw gathered at my feet, the people glow with anticipation.

Smiling slyly and weightless, I rise off the platform. Fools, to think these ropes could hold me.

MEG CAVEN

To Surviving Members of the Family

Ms. Sarah Luciani, 28, requests the honor

of your presence

at a reading of the last will of her husband

Adolpho Dominico Luciani

recently deceased at 89.

Family Estate,

Montauk, New York,

Sunday, June 6,

Noon.

Black tie and bodyguard optional.

Reception following services.

Moving vans unnecessary.

Firearms prohibited.

RSVP by phone.

LAURA JARRETT

THE ARRIVAL OF THE GHOST

As soon as it happened, I rushed home to tell my wife the bad news. But she wouldn't listen to me. She looked right through me and poured herself another drink. Turned on Letterman.

Then the phone rang. She picked it up.

I watched her face crumble, heard her wail of grief.

CHARLES ENRIGHT

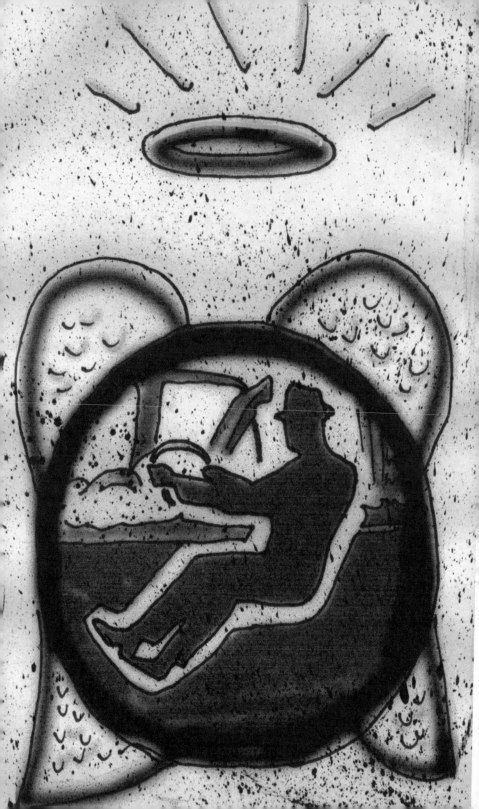

He Auto Know Better

"No, Jill!" he snapped. "I don't trust you!"

They walked towards their garage as Joe pointed his cane at his restored Studebaker.

Jill teases his face with her hair—dazzling red covering gray—and, shifting her voice to sexy, low, cooed: "Joe, my darling! Be an angel. Let me drive today."

He did.

He is.

WALT JOHLER

WELCOME HOME

Squeezing through the late morning fog, suddenly sunlight smacks my face. Today, I finally meet my grandfather. Dew seeps into these wandering boots.

"Ah, here. . ."

He's pitted, worn, and covered in moss, but I see him clearly.

William Reginald Smith III, Born 1809, Died 1890.

"Hello, Grandpa. It's me, Christopher."

SEAN CHRISTOPHER

HARRY'S FRIENDS

Everybody knew Harry. Loved him. Why had it happened? I hear an affair. No, financial. No, it was his health. Who knows. They said the rope was brand new. Wife found him in the morning. Hanging is the grimmest. Terrible thing, really. Just terrible. Have you tried the paté? Everyone knew Harry. Loved him.

DARYL M. WOODS

EARTH POKER

Cigar smoke wafted through the firmament. The players tossed their chips into the pot.

Jesus gambled on Ireland. Adonai bet Israel. Shiva wagered India. Allah risked Iran.

"Show your cards."

Straight flushes, ace high, all around. Laughter thundered, filling the heavens; life sparked throughout the universe.

"Whose deal?"

JULIE TARDOS

FREE FROM HIDING

Sinking the blade deeper, rupturing the wall of my heart, finally I could feel pain, my entire life's pain, and it poured out, thickly red.

This long abysmal cry softened to a dark sleep as ancient memories emerged from inner hidden dormancy. I sensed this time would be my last attempt. Somehow, it was all right.

SEAN CHRISTOPHER

WELCOME TO GRACELAND

Yesterday I caught a cold and went to bed with a temperature of 105. But this morning, I feel great.

I went for a heavenly walk, and who should I bump into but Elvis.

"Hey," I said. "I knew you weren't dead."

"Guess again," he said.

"But how on earth—"

"My point exactly," he explained.

TAYLOR BINGHAM

MODERN MEDICINE

Blinding headlights, deafening crash, searing pain, absolute blackness, then the warm, welcoming, clear blue light, irresistibly beckoning. John felt gloriously happy, youthful, and free as he strolled into the enveloping radiance.

Slowly, the pain and darkness returned. John's swollen eyes agonizingly opened—bandages, tubes, casts, both legs missing, his tearful wife.

"They saved you, Honey!"

AUGUST SALEMI

I Want to Speak to the Management

He had been born to money and privilege. Power and fame both followed him. He grew accustomed to people rushing to fulfill his every whim.

Yet now, to his dismay, he was being denied absolutely.

"I'm sorry," came the answer. "You have no reservations here."

And with that, Saint Peter closed the Pearly Gates.

DAVID KIRKLAND

Stories We Loved and Were Dying to Include

* * *

TIME'S UP

"Oh, no!"

"What?"

"You've accidentally turned the time machine on! It's going into the past!"

"Quick! Flip the 'RETURN' switch!"

"It's stuck! Now we're really screwed!"

"God! It's trapped in a 55-second time loop! Can things get any worse?"

"Oh, no!"

"What?"

"You've accidentally turned the time machine on! It's going into the past—"

ENRIQUE S. ANADANA

CONFLUENCE

The well was on top of the hill, of all places! We grabbed a pail and went on up there. At the summit, there were other folks milling around. A chick with a shepherd's crook, a fragile-looking guy, and an arachnophobe.

"We seem to be in the wrong rhyme," a nerd in blue explained.

DAVID CROSSLAND

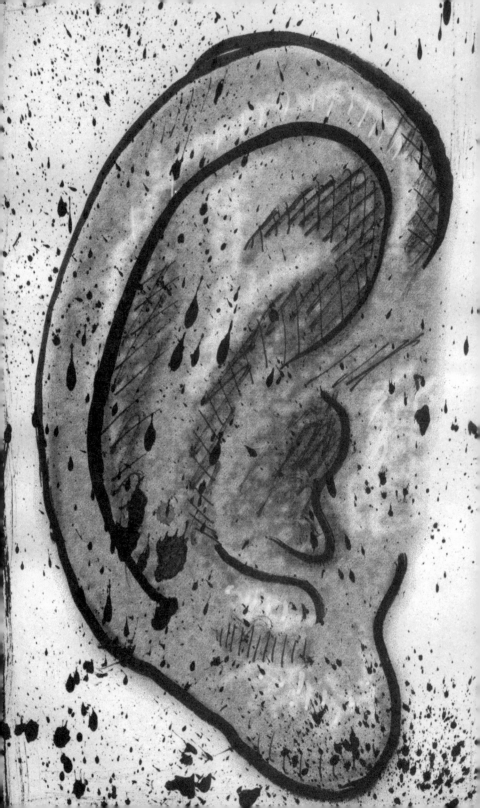

HEAR NO EVIL

"You're free to go!" Judge Hardy shouts at Clements, who bolts from the courtroom, leaving his twelve peers frozen with disbelief in the jury box.

His ashen-faced lawyer finds him kissing the courtroom steps.

"Do you believe it?" says Clements. "Not freakin' guilty!"

In chambers, Judge Hardy fits a new battery into his hearing aid.

ROB AUSTIN

THE FORTUNE TELLER

"I see grave misfortune," said the gypsy, gazing into her crystal ball.

"Do you know what's . . . going to happen?" replied the man in a nervous whisper.

"I see a gun, and someone you know stealing your wallet."

"But how can you be so certain? How?"

The gypsy raised her gun and smiled.

SANDY STOSIC

THE SEARCH

Finally, in this remote village, his quest ended.

There, by the fire, sat Truth.

Never had he seen an older, uglier woman.

"Are you Truth?"

The wizened, wrinkled hag nodded.

"What message can I take from you to the world?" he pleaded.

She replied, spitting into the fire, "Tell them I am young and beautiful."

ROBERT TOMPKINS

EVERYTHING THAT'S HAPPENED

A whirl of gas congeals into a sphere, and the ground yields heavy lizards. They roam, eat plants, then sink into the dirt. Monkeys fall from the trees, build homes from rocks, and float on the waters. They invent guns and books, draw borders, watch a Ford Bronco on the freeway.

That's about it, so far.

MICHAEL KIRCHHOFF

UNLEASHED TONGUE

Bob taught his dog to talk.

Buster's first phrases were simple. "Want food." "Need go outside." Eventually, the two would stay up all night discussing the wonders of life.

One day, Buster voiced his displeasure with the pet/master hierarchy. Bob refused to relinquish the leash.

Buster never spoke again, choosing instead to bark incessantly.

KURT VAVRA

PUBLISHED

March. Small cyclones in the concrete canyons, twirling trash like dervishes.

"Two men were arrested. . . " he types, then stops, gazing out the window. A smile.

"The difference," he thinks, "between journalism and writing a book, is that on a windy day, you don't see a bunch of books swirling around in the street."

NEIL STEINBERG

THE RAREST OF ALL

"Forty-two million exactly."

Sir Michael took the check and gingerly handed over the ancient vase.

"You've finally won, Langston. You now have the only two left in the world."

"Yes, but what I really wanted," Langston replied, smashing the vase into a thousand pieces on the floor, "was the only one in the world."

JOHN GERACI

55 WORDS THAT
CHANGED MY LIFE

Using a free newspaper to keep warm, I noticed a story contest. Entered and won.

The *New Yorker* republished my story. I got a book contract from Knopf. Pulitzer, Spielberg deal, yadda, yadda.

I bought the Waldorf Astoria and housed the homeless.

I give them free newspapers to keep warm.

Hey, it worked for me.

KATHERINE WILDE

AND THE HORSE
THEY RODE IN ON

They called it "Tourette's Syndrome," this need to

shout obscenities. He thought they were full of

_____, that they could all go _____ them-

selves. Bunch of no good _____ who should

_____ and _____ , then

_____ and _____ _____ and

_____ _____ and then _____

_____ _____ _____ ___.

But why did he feel this way?

Maybe there was something missing in his life.

Oh, _____ it, he thought.

WILLIAM S. HOWE

FROM THE DIRECTOR'S CHAIR

The director sits mulling over his dilemma.

Mr. Rostein had just called from Hollywood, upset that film production was already eight million over.

What to do...?

Suddenly, a knock on his trailer door.

"Lunch ready?"

"Yes, sir, your favorite—lobster and filet mignon."

Wetting his lips, the director thinks "God, do I love this job!"

TODD THOMPSON

NO PROSPECT AT THE END

In The Beginning, there was The Word, followed by The Sentence, followed by The Paragraph, followed by The Short Story, followed by The Novel, followed by The Sequel.

God read all The Words, declared them Good, and then created The Title for all His Best-Sellers: "The Never-Ending Story."

MICHAEL DRIVER

DEED IS DONE

The sharp blade cut through tender flesh . . . stiletto thin, hard, and cold. Deft jabs, so precise; no mistakes, clever cuts. Careful work in the dark of night.

Arms tire. Slimy hands. Such a mess! Clean up quick—wrap the ooze, wipe the knife. . .

Set it on the porch for Halloween.

Now light the candle!

HOLLY ZIEGLER

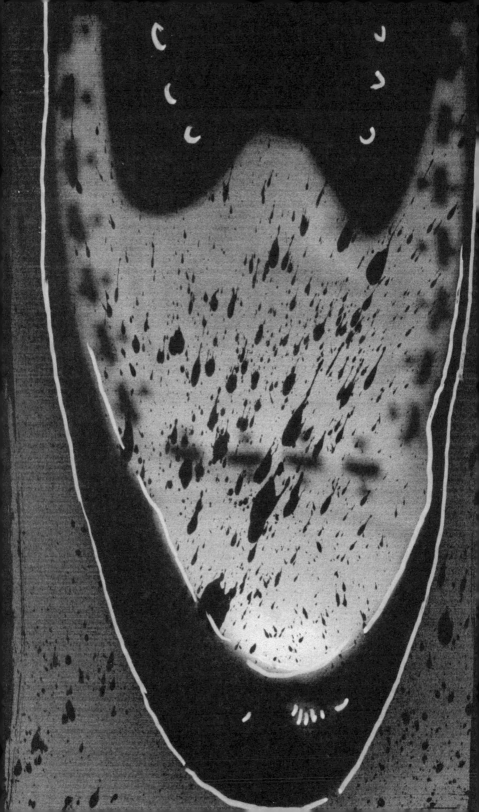

ELVIS IN THE WINGS

"They're gonna love you tender, son. They'll love you to death."

"I cain't go out there, Colonel."

"S'matter, boy? You all shook up?"

"I cain't do it."

"Don't be cruel, son. It's now or never."

"I cain't, Colonel. I just cain't move!"

"You old hound dog, why?"

"'Cause you're standin' on my blue suede shoes!"

THOMAS PARKER

BACK IN TIME

"Your theory about time is wrong," he said. "Yes, the time machine worked, but in Salzburg I changed nothing."

"Let's take a break and consider our options," she said. "Let's have dinner before the concert. They're performing Mozart's 50th Symphony."

"As long as there's no Beethoven," he said. "I can't stand him."

"Who?" she asked.

JEFF BAKER AND JOHN BOGNER

SILENCE IS GOLDEN

The two boys pushed the branch aside to get a clearer view of the old women standing around the steaming black pot.

"Witches!"

"Ah, c'mon—are not!"

"They're stirring a caldron over a fire!"

"Maybe it's a campout."

"They're talking weird!"

"Foreigners."

"Witches!"

"Are not!"

"Are too!"

"Not!"

POOF!

"Ribit!"

"Told ya!"

POOF!

"Ribit!"

PAT HOEFFLER

As Time Goes By

"At last!" cried Huttmeyer.

In his hand he held a small vial containing the results of 60 years' research—memory elixir. He swallowed and his mind was flooded with the past . . . a lifetime of solitude in the laboratory . . . loneliness, frustration, failure upon failure.

Sobbing in his hands, he wracked his mind for an antidote.

KURT VAVRA

PLACE TITLE HERE

(A) Setup, premise, introduction. Describe situation, perhaps in line(s) of dialogue. May introduce primary character.

(B) Response to (A), modifying, affirming, or negating above. May introduce secondary character, possibly by means of additional dialogue.

(C) Moral, resolution, ironic twist. May pose rhetorical question or express despair. Often compromised by dwindling availability of words.

BILL CROWN

55 fiction

The Rules

* * *

How To Write
A 55-Word Story

Just about everyone who reads the diminutive stories in this book eventually tries writing one, too—which is why we've included this handy set of official Fifty-Five Fiction rules so you'll know exactly how to go about it when the urge strikes.

So What's a Story, Anyway?

In the first place, remember we're talking fiction here, not essays or poems or errant thoughts. Although some people in the rarefied upper regions of literary endeavor may have a more complex and creative definition of just what constitutes a "story," for our purposes back down here, a story is a story only if it contains the following four elements: 1) a setting; 2) a character or characters; 3) conflict; and 4) resolution.

For those of you who think this is somehow overly academic or perhaps creatively limiting, consider for a moment that:

1) All stories have to be happening some place, which means they have to have a setting of some kind, even if it's the other side of the universe, the inner reaches of someone's mind, or just the house next door.

2) Characters can have infinite variations. People, animals, rocks, microbes. Anything.

3) By conflict, we merely mean that in the course of the story, something has to happen. The lovers argue. The deer flees. The astronauts wait in anticipation. Even in this last example, something is happening, even though no one is moving or talking. There is conflict, which leads us to:

4) The outcome of the story, known by English teachers as resolution. This doesn't necessarily mean that there's a moral ("Justice is its own reward," "In the end, love triumphs"), or even that the conflict itself is resolved. It may or may not be.

But what it does mean is that when the story ends, someone has to have learned something (He found out his wife wanted to kill him after all; they'd successfully eluded the enemy when they thought they'd been discovered; Jim was shown to be as much of a liar as his father; whatever). It's even possible to have none of the characters learn anything. If that's the case, then we the reader must.

Again, we can't stress enough the importance of making certain you're writing a story, so examine your work honestly and carefully. A lot of well-written entries have often contained intriguing characters in situations with nothing happening. And some people send poems which, though great as poetry, fail as stories.

A Few Words About Your Few Words

Other important points to keep in mind:

• You can write about anything you like, but you can't use more than 55 words.

• If it's in the dictionary, it's a word. No matter how short.

• Hyphenated words can't count as single words. Compound adjectives like "dyed-in-the-wool commie," "long-time friend," etc. are good examples. If you take away the hyphens, they're clearly made up of multiple words. Exceptions to this are any words that don't become two complete free-standing words when the hyphen is removed. For example, "re" isn't a word when the hyphen is taken from "re-entry," but "entry" is.

• Also, please note that your story's title isn't included in the word count. But remember, too, that it can't be more than seven words long. We had one wise guy submit a story whose title was twice the length of his story, and we were not amused. At least, not at the time.

• Contractions count as single words, so if you're really seeking word economy (as you should be), keep this in mind. If you write "He will jump," it's three words. But if you write "He'll jump," it's only two. Very economical. By the same token, any contraction that's a shortened form of a word is also counted as a full word. Using 'em for "them" comes to mind.

• An initial also counts as a word (L.L. Bean, e.e. cummings, etc.) since it's basically an abbreviation of a full word. The only exception is when it's part of an acronym like MGM, NASA, or IBM. Our reasoning here is that the wide-spread use of the initials as acronyms has in effect made them into a single word.

• Remember that numbers count as words, too, expressed as either numerals (8, 28, 500, or 1984), or as words (eight, twenty-eight, etc.). But keep in mind our hyphenated word rule. Twenty-eight is two words when written out, but only one when expressed as 28. Don't cheat yourself out of an extra word that you may need.

• Any punctuation is allowed, and none count as words, so don't worry about being miserly with them if they work to some effect.

• Jokes just don't cut it. In the past, we've tried to weed out stories that are actually just old jokes re-written in a 55-word format, but occasionally one slips by and someone eventually points it out to us, much to our embarrassment. We're wiser now, so proceed down this path at your peril.

• You can submit as many stories as you want, but—each story must be submitted (preferably typed) on its own sheet of paper. Make sure your name, address, and telephone number are included on each story submission so we can contact you should you be one of our winners. That means if you send us 10 stories on 10 separate sheets of paper, this information needs to be with each one in case they get separated. We've been unable to contact too many authors of great stories simply because they forgot this simple procedure.

ONE FINAL WORD

To be considered for our next book, put a stamp on that envelope and mail your story off to us at Fifty-Five Fiction, 197 Santa Rosa St., San Luis Obispo, CA 93449.

And remember: Just 55 words. ❊

ABOUT THE EDITORS

Steve Moss is the editor and publisher of *New Times*, an alternative weekly newspaper that he founded in San Luis Obispo, California, and where 55 Fiction began as an annual writing contest. He grew up in Southern California and attended Brooks Institute, UC Santa Barbara, and Syracuse University, where he studied the visual arts, but eventually switched to journalism because journalists were more fun to hang out with.

He's been a reporter, editor, busboy, art director, advertising copywriter, and graphic artist and enjoyed all of them except the busboy stuff.

His other works include *The World's Shortest Stories* (editor), *The Book of the Few* (editor), *GroanerZ* (editor), *The Coffee Book, Inconsequential Journeys, Memories & Misdemeanors* (editor), and *The I Chew*.

If he could write another book, he would. And probably will.

John M. Daniel was born in Minnesota, raised in Texas, and educated in Massachusetts. He was a Wallace Stegner Fellow in Creative Writing at Stanford University and a writer in residence at Wilbur Hot Springs. He has taught fiction at UCLA Extension, Santa Barbara Adult Education, the Santa Barbara Writer's Conference, and elsewhere.

His short stories have appeared in numerous literary magazines, from Aberrations to ZYZZYVA. He is the author of a mystery novel, *Play Melancholy Baby*; a cat book, *The Love Story of Sushi and Sashimi*; a short story collection, *The Woman by the Bridge*; a memoir, *One for the Books: Confessions of a Small Press Publisher*; and a writing handbook, *Structure, Style, and Truth—Elements of the Short Story*.

He has worked as a bookseller, freelance writer, editor, entertainer, model, innkeeper, and teacher. He is now a small-press publisher in Santa Barbara, California.

The World's Shortest Stories

Edited by Steve Moss

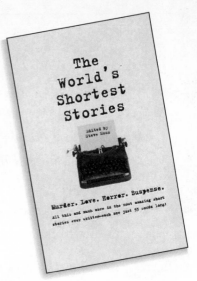

Murder. Love. Horror. Suspense.

All This and Much More in the Most Amazing Short Stories Ever Written—Each One Just 55 Words Long!

* * *

A compilation of the best entries in the annual Fifty-Five Fiction writing contest held by New Times in San Luis Obispo, this volume offers more than 150 masterpieces of brevity in writing! Enjoy mysteries, love stories, and creepy ironies in less time than it takes to tie your shoe.

$7.95 / $11.95 CAN paperback
ISBN 0-7624-0300-4

"Concise yarns . . . filled with energy and verve."
—Los Angeles Times